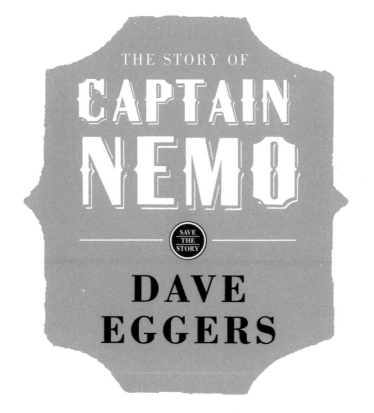

THE STORY OF

# CAPTAIN NEMO

SAVE THE STORY

## DAVE EGGERS

ILLUSTRATED BY FABIAN NEGRIN

PUSHKIN CHILDREN'S BOOKS

Pushkin Children's Books
71–75 Shelton Street
London WC2H 9JQ

*The Story of Captain Nemo* first published in Italian as *La storia di Capitano Nemo*

© 2011 Gruppo Editoriale L'Espresso S.p.A
and © 2011 Dave Eggers. All rights reserved.

This edition published by Pushkin Children's Books in 2013

ISBN 978 1 782690 18 4

Set in Garamond Premier Pro by Tetragon, London

Printed and bound in Italy by Printer Trento SRL
on Munken Print Cream 115gsm

www.pushkinpress.com

# THE STORY OF
# CAPTAIN NEMO

*One*

My name is Consuelo. You probably heard something about what happened to me and the others on the ship called the *Abraham Lincoln*. Well, whatever you heard was pretty much completely wrong. I'll tell you the truth.

This happened last summer, when I was fourteen. My uncle, Pierre Arronax, is French and has been pretty much everywhere. He's a well-known oceanographer, which basically means he gets to go where he wants to and do whatever he wants to do, as long as it's underwater. If he wants to look into some shipwreck from 2,000 years ago, he can do that. If he wants to see how deep the Marianas Trench is, he can do that. If he wants to learn how to talk to killer whales, someone will pay him to try. He's got a pretty good job.

Last year he called me up and asked me what I was doing for summer break. I said I wasn't

sure. I told him I probably had a job at the local supermarket, bagging groceries, but nothing was set in stone. I live in Nebraska, in an area called the Badlands, and though the name sounds fascinating and even dangerous, it's anything but. It's probably the most boring place in the world. I had a feeling Uncle Pierre had an idea for me to get out of town for a while, so I said I was free.

"Well," he said, "I need an assistant to come along with me on a trip. A bunch of ships have been sunk by what seems to be a sea creature larger and more powerful than any in recorded history, and I thought we'd look into it. Want to come?"

I packed my things.

I took a train from Omaha to New York, and then a taxi over the Brooklyn Bridge. When I got to the pier where I was supposed to meet Uncle Pierre, a dozen men were loading the *Abraham Lincoln*, a cross between a fishing ship and some kind of military destroyer. It was equipped with ten cannon-style harpoon guns, acres of industrial-strength nets, various small guns and artillery cannons and six torpedo chutes. It was built to fight anyone and anything.

"Hello there!" a voice said. I looked up. I knew that accent anywhere—it was my Uncle Pierre. It had been a year since I'd seen him, and he had a new scar. He always had a new scar. This one was on his neck, where, he said, he'd been slashed by a stingray. If the tail had hit him just a fraction off, it would have killed him. Otherwise, though, he looked like a professor—a delicate one, too. He was tall, thin and wore thick wire-rimmed glasses.

"How are you, boy?" he asked me, and punched me in the shoulder. That's his way of greeting. I told him I was fine, punched him back and asked him if we'd really be seeing some kind of unknown sea monster. I was sceptical, I have to admit. I was sceptical and scared and excited all at once.

"I'll tell you all about it later," he said. "Get on board, drop your stuff off and I'll see you at dinner."

I was left alone all afternoon as the ship left New York. From the stern I watched the city shrink from view, and soon we were in open water. The surf was rough and it had been a while since I'd been on a ship, so I puked on and off for the first few hours. The joys of the sea!

I wasn't hungry at dinner time, but at six I sat down with Uncle Pierre and the officers of the *Abe Lincoln*. There were men and women from all over the world—South Africa, Sweden, New Zealand and England and Italy and Lebanon. It was a truly international and fascinating crew, and I can't describe them all here. But there were two men who should be mentioned: one was the Captain himself, whose name was Farragut. He was an American of about fifty years old, and seemed a very solid, no-nonsense type with a giant black moustache. He took the job of finding the monster very seriously. The second man of note was a huge Canadian named Ned Land, a world-class killer of whales and all large ocean mammals. He'd been a whaler for thirty years, and every battle and every kill seemed to show on his face. His hair was red, his complexion ruddy and his mouth a mess of broken and missing teeth.

Between the two of them, I got the low-down on the creature we'd be hunting.

"You don't know this, because they've been keeping it out of the news," Uncle Pierre said, "but something has been sinking all kinds of ships in the oceans all over the world. You remember that Russian fishing boat that was found near the Bering Strait?"

I nodded. I remembered that a few months before there was something in the news about a large industrial fishing boat washing ashore.

"I knew those men," Captain Farragut said, and looked down at his plate.

"At least ten men missing," Ned Land said. "All presumed dead."

"Well, that was the first strange occurrence," Uncle Pierre continued. "After that, there have been sightings and incidents all over the place—in the Pacific, the Indian Ocean, all across the Atlantic. At least six ships have been sunk under mysterious circumstances. Some sailors, just before abandoning ship, reported seeing massive phosphorescence on the surface of the water. Others are sure it was some kind of submarine. But it moves far too fast and is much too big to be a submarine. So now everyone's convinced it's a sea creature, a giant squid perhaps. But if it's a squid, it's bigger and stronger than anything ever seen."

"Might be a bunch of 'em," Ned added.

I almost spat out my carrot juice. A bunch of giant squids, taking down ships all over the globe? Why would they do that? Where would they have come from? I asked Uncle Pierre a slew of questions. He answered patiently.

"Since the northern oceans have been warming, scientists have been finding squids of unbelievable size, washed up and floating on the surface of the water. The assumption is that as the oceans are warming, their food supply is changing or dying, and so they're dying, too. And they're migrating, looking for new homes, new food sources. So suddenly these creatures that usually occupied the lowest reaches of the oceans are visible. And they might be so desperate for food that they're attacking anything they see."

I must have looked sceptical, because Uncle Pierre became defensive. "You know I'm no crackpot, right, Con?"

Uncle Pierre called me Con, which I liked a lot better than Connie, the name my other relatives called me. I don't know about your language, but in English, in Nebraska especially, Connie is a woman's name.

Anyway, I agreed with Uncle Pierre that he wasn't a crackpot. He was considered by the scientific community to be sane, careful about his work and the statements he made publicly. He never announced a discovery or a theory until he was absolutely sure he could back it up. So the fact that he thought it possible that giant squids were terrorizing the oceans got me excited, and a little scared, too.

"OK," I said, "there's a giant squid—"

"Or maybe dozens of them—" Ned corrected.

"Right," I added. "There may be dozens of them, bigger and stronger than anything that we've ever seen before. And they're out there sinking fishing boats all over the ocean. And we're in a fishing boat, about to go look for them?"

"Exactly," Pierre said, seeming relieved I'd finally understood.

"But what's stopping this squid from sinking us, too?" I asked.

"Nothing at all," he said.

"Nothing but me," Ned Land said. He locked eyes with me. "Don't you worry, son. Whatever it is that's been killing the sailors, I will kill it."

Two

I closed my eyes that night and imagined squids the size of buses, their tentacles a mile long, dragging us down to the bottom of the sea. I'd seen squids move before, on YouTube, and I knew they were equipped with incredible speed and agility. They could disappear in the blink of an eye, capture prey like a flash of lightning. If Ned Land was used to hunting whales, he would be no match for a squid of the same size. I didn't sleep well that night or any night on the *Abraham Lincoln*.

Luckily, that first week I didn't need to be well rested. Nothing much happened. The first objective was to search the seas near Greenland, where the monster had last been seen. Apparently there had just been an attack on a large fishing ship there, and five men had been lost. The ocean around was sky blue and dotted with icebergs, and immediately I wondered just how a giant squid would survive in water so cold. The squid or squids had been spotted in the Indian Ocean, too, which was surely about fifty degrees warmer than the water here. What kind of animal could withstand that kind of change in temperature? I didn't ask Uncle Pierre. I was always afraid a question would be too silly to ask, its answer too obvious.

So we headed to the western coast of Greenland and arrived at Port Nuuk. We docked, and Uncle Pierre took me to talk to the locals for a while. They hadn't seen the attack, but the hull of the ship had been recovered, and we saw that it had been punctured three times—each on the starboard side. Every puncture was triangular in shape, about eighteen inches in diameter. The hull of the ship was iron, six inches thick. I couldn't imagine what kind of beast could break through such a wall.

Pierre did some calculations. "The force it would take to puncture the hull would be the equivalent of a truck driving at 200 miles per hour."

"It couldn't have been a squid," Ned Land said.

"You're right," Pierre said. "Are you thinking what I'm thinking?"

"I think I am. I'm thinking narwhal," Ned said.

"Yup, narwhal."

"What's a narwhal?" I asked.

Uncle Pierre explained that a narwhal is a large ocean mammal, related to but a bit bigger than a dolphin—about the size of a beluga whale. Like the beluga, it has smooth, milky white skin, but particular to the narwhal is a long horn extending from its head, sometimes as long as five feet.

"Unicorn of the sea," Ned said, and looked again at the punctures in the side of the ship's hull, as if wondering what I was wondering—whether the narwhal's horn was strong enough to do such a thing.

"If this was done by a narwhal," Uncle Pierre said, "its horn would have to be about ten times larger than any horn we've ever recovered."

"And strong enough to puncture iron six inches thick," I noted.

"At ten times the size of a standard horn, it could be strong enough," Pierre said. "And if the narwhal drove itself at maximum speed... Hm." It was as if he were doubting the probability, even while explaining it.

"Whatever it is," Ned concluded, "we'll kill it."

And so we left Greenland and made for the next place the beast had been sighted—off the coast of Nova Scotia. The trip took us three days in rough weather, the ocean grey and churning. The morale of the crew lagged. Everyone was grumpy, and the constant rocking of the ship kept me throwing up continuously. I don't think I kept anything in my stomach for more than twelve minutes at a stretch. Meanwhile, Ned Land was furious that we were pursuing the monster this way.

"What, the beast is just waiting in the spot of the last attack?" he bellowed. To him it made no sense, particularly for a creature whose attacks had spanned the globe, from the coast of Argentina to Franz Josef Land. "Why would it attack and just wait for us to arrive? There's no logic in it."

I have to admit that I agreed with Ned. The beast's attacks were all over the world, and it

seemed to move quickly from one to the next—
no two attacks were ever in the same place. But
Captain Farragut stuck to the plan.

"These are our orders," he said.

So we continued this way for another two weeks.
Every time we would get word of another sighting
of the monster, we would set sail for that place,
and of course by the time we got there the monster
would be half a world away, sinking another ship.
When we were in the Caribbean, it was near Brazil.

When we were in Brazil, it was near the Antarctic. By now we had been gone almost a month and the crew were restless. Most of the time was spent so far from land that we couldn't even see a bird or smell any sign of civilization. During the day, we would take turns sitting in the crow's nest, looking for some sign of the monster. Or rather, they took turns. No one trusted me to do anything. I was bored silly, and started thinking that, by comparison, life in Nebraska was pretty exciting.

Still, we kept chasing it—to Nova Scotia, to Iceland, to the coast of Spain and finally to West Africa, where an enormous ship had recently been attacked.

There had been 120 men and women on board, and only 90 had survived. By the time we got to the coast of Senegal, as usual we saw no sign of the beast. When we docked in Dakar, we saw the remains of a ship that had been punctured just days before. This fishing ship had been struck, but not sunk, by the monster. The crew described the beast coming at them, ramming the hull repeatedly, puncturing it with a long, horn-like appendage. This seemed to confirm that the beast was indeed some kind of super-narwhal.

The crew of this ship had been lucky, in that the attack had taken place in relatively shallow waters; and they had watched as the creature, once within sight of the city, had retreated as if it were shy, as if it didn't want to be seen in the light of day. A few of the citizens of Dakar had seen it from the tall buildings in the town centre. They confirmed that it seemed to notice it was visible, and then quickly disappeared underwater.

"An agoraphobic mass-murdering sea monster?" Ned asked.

"At this point," my uncle said, "it makes as much sense as anything else."

Just then a crew member arrived at the Captain's side with urgent news. The monster had been sighted just a hundred miles south. We rushed to the *Abe Lincoln* and made off immediately.

# Three

We sailed all afternoon and in the evening arrived at the co-ordinates where a small fishing vessel had reported seeing the creature. The night was exceptionally dark—no moon, no stars. And, as usual, there was no sign of the beast.

Until there was.

A spotter in the crow's nest screamed out the news: "Captain! There's something right in front of us!"

The entire crew of the ship ran towards the bow: the Captain, the officers, the masters, sailors and cabin boys—even the men from the engine room. Everyone assembled and stared into the darkness, trying to see what the harpooner was seeing. The Captain radioed back to the ship's control room.

"You see anything on the radar?"

"Negative," the technician said.

Whatever this thing was, it wasn't showing up anywhere. We all stared into the dark sea, looking for any sign of movement. The dark was absolute.

It seemed impossible that anything, no matter how big, could be seen in such blackness.

But then I saw it, because it began emitting light. It started as a dull underwater glow, then grew like a blanket of light on the surface of the water. The honey-coloured luminescence revealed the creature's shape—a vast oval mass of at least 200 feet. It was about 500 feet in front of us, and seemed to be directing itself towards the *Abe Lincoln* like a missile.

"What do we do?" one of the crew members asked.

Farragut seemed speechless.

"I know what I'm going to do," Ned Land said, "I'm gonna get that rocket launcher and blow that thing out of the water."

"No," Farragut said. "Wait at least to see how it moves."

We didn't have to wait long. As if it had heard Farragut's suggestion, it suddenly accelerated directly towards our ship. It picked up speed until it was going about fifty miles an hour. It seemed inevitable that it would strike us. And if it struck us, we would sink. I glanced over my shoulder, looking for the closest lifeboat.

But just as it was about to hit us, it didn't. Like the most agile fish, it suddenly swung around us and in milliseconds had passed the ship—like a stick in a stream whipping around an embedded stone.

I couldn't believe it. It was faster than anything I'd ever seen in the ocean. The only thing comparable was a swordfish. It was faster than any shark, any barracuda. By now it was far beyond us, about a mile away, though we could still see it. It had left a phosphorescent trail in the sea. Then, as if allowing us to catch up, it paused.

Our ship sped up, and gave chase. And for the next fourteen hours we continued this way. We chased the creature for what must have been 300 miles. We chased it at thirty knots and twenty knots and fifteen. We watched as it raced away from us at speeds far greater than we could attain, and then slow down, as if it were testing our speed and, having found our limits, let us catch up. We watched it disappear under the surface of the water, only to reappear ten minutes later, spouting water a hundred feet into the air. We chased it through that first night and throughout the next morning and afternoon. The day would have been filled with the thrill of the hunt, and something of the fun of watching a playful animal—but we knew that, at any moment, the monster might turn on us and attack us directly. What was it waiting for, anyway?

We found out soon enough. The sun had set, and we were somewhere in the middle of the Atlantic. The creature's phosphorescence again overtook the surface of the water. If I hadn't known better, I'd have thought the monster didn't want to be seen too close-up in the light of day—just as it hadn't wanted to be seen too close to the city of Dakar. But as the darkness of night grew thicker, the monster let us gain on it. It was travelling south at about fifteen knots, and we were gaining steadily. With every league gained, Ned grew more excited. He positioned himself behind the giant harpoon—a cannon that could shoot a harpoon the speed of a bullet and with far more damage.

"Come on!" he yelled. "Just a little closer!"

Finally we were within striking range.

"Yah!" Ned yelled as he fired the first harpoon.

It shot out from the ship with the force of a missile, and it was right on target. It struck the creature precisely in the middle of the back, and in

the spray of surf I couldn't immediately see what
happened, but I heard a loud thwack. I was sure that
it had hit the monster, and must have punctured
its skin. It was a horrible sound, a sound like a car
crash, a sound like death.

But when the spray cleared, there was no sign
of the harpoon. There was only the wire extended
sadly into the ocean, dragging through the waves.

"What happened?" I asked.

"Bounced right off," Farragut said.

"Couldn't have," Ned said.

"Speed up." Farragut ordered the ship to pursue
the monster again, and soon enough we were
within firing range again. And again Ned shot his

harpoon at jet-plane speed, directly at the monster.
And again, when the spray cleared, the harpoon had
done no damage at all. There was barely a scratch on
the surface.

Everyone on board was dumbfounded. We all
looked at each other, wondering what the next
move was. Maybe a torpedo? Maybe a rocket
launcher?

We didn't have much time to think about it,
though, because just then the monster turned
around, quick as a dolphin, and before we could
yell "Look out!!" it had rammed our ship. It was
if the world's axis had been thrown upwards. I
found myself sliding backwards down the deck,

hitting ropes, chairs, a duct. The crew were flailing everywhere, trying to recover. A series of reports and commands flew about.

"It's broken the rudder!" "The engine's damaged!"

Small fires broke out all over. The ship rocked and swayed wildly, and when it momentarily righted itself, I was flung overboard.

Four

Thirty feet down, and then I was in the Atlantic. It was cold, the waves were roiling and, being from Nebraska, I'm not the best swimmer in the world. All I could hear was the engine of the *Abe Lincoln*, which was steaming out of range—though it no doubt wanted to stay, to rescue whomever was overboard, it had no choice but to steam on, rudderless.

I treaded water, looking for any scrap of wood to grab onto. But there was nothing, and I couldn't see more than a few feet in front of me anyway. There were sharks in these waters, I knew, and I expected one of my legs to be ripped off at any moment in the jaws of a great white.

I didn't expect to live long.

Then I heard a voice.

"Consuelo! Consuelo!"

It was my Uncle Pierre.

"Where are you?" I called out.

"Over here. Follow my voice."

He continued to call out, and I swam towards the sound. It was so dark that I bumped into him before I saw him.

"Thank God you're alive and OK," he said. "Your parents would have killed me."

I've been happy to see Uncle Pierre many times in my life, but I was never as happy to see him as I was that night. Without him I would have drowned for sure.

"You'd better take off your clothes," he said.

See, I didn't know that. I didn't know that if you're fully clothed, and trying to survive in the mid-Atlantic at night, you should take off your clothes. I did, and instantly I was fifty pounds lighter.

Uncle Pierre was holding onto a life preserver that had fallen from the ship when it was upended by the monster, and we took turns holding onto it for an hour or so. All the while I was still terrified that at any moment we'd become a meal for a shark or killer whale. Just then we heard another voice, the voice that would save both our lives.

"Anyone out there?"

It was Ned Land.

Again we used our voices to find each other. We swam towards Ned, and soon found him. Or his silhouette at least. It was not floating in the water, as we were. Instead, Ned seemed to be sitting atop a kind of rock.

"What is that?" I asked.

He was matter-of-fact. "This is the beast."

Uncle Pierre and I were flabbergasted. We assumed that the monster and *Abe Lincoln* were many miles away by then, continuing their battle. Instead, the beast was still here, and standing stock-still?

"I know this is it," Ned said. "I never forget the hide of a sea monster. This is the thing I harpooned. This is the thing that attacked us. Get aboard."

We abandoned our life preserver and climbed on. The thing was hard as stone, and rose about three feet from the water's surface. We straddled it as you would the back of a horse. It was evident that this was just the thing's back, and we were aboard its spine. Normally I would have been terrified to be on top of a creature that had killed so many, but I was so exhausted and happy to be out of the water that I felt strangely grateful.

"Wait," I said, finally noticing the surface. "This isn't an animal. It's not organic. This is metal."

"Yes. I noticed that," Ned said, as if I'd finally spotted something fairly obvious.

Uncle Pierre had been inspecting it, too. "It's some kind of submarine."

Ned and Uncle Pierre put their deductions together. It was apparently a man-made vessel that had been doing all the damage around the globe. The implications were hard to comprehend, but they made a bit more sense. After all, persecution was a human speciality. What animal would have hunted ship after ship, as if by design? Now that we knew it was a human endeavour it seemed to add up.

"I hate to interrupt you two," I said, "but what happens if this thing goes under?"

"Good point," Ned said, and began pounding on the exterior of the machine. It made about as much noise as hitting the side of a skyscraper with a rubber chicken. But we had no choice but to try. For the next two hours, all three of us walked up and down the length of the submarine, stomping, pounding and screaming.

"Wait. What happens if they let us in?" I asked.

"What do you mean?" Uncle Pierre said.

"I mean, aren't they the ones who have sunk half a dozen ships and tried to sink ours last night? What makes you think they won't just kill us?"

Ned had an answer. "If we spend any more time in the Atlantic, we're dead anyway. Look!"

In the distance I could make out low, triangular shapes rising from the surface of the sea. "Are those sharks?" I asked.

"They're not pandas," Ned replied.

So we went back to pounding. The sharks grew closer, and began circling. There were at least four of them, and they seemed to be assessing their plan of attack. I imagined them underwater, choosing which of them got which one of us. They were divvying us up, licking their shark chops.

And just when they seemed to have decided who would eat whom and how, there was a hissing sound at the aft end of the submarine. A portal opened and, quick as a swarm of bees leaving their hive, eight men, all of them in black, armed with bizarre weapons, had surrounded us, shoved us through the portal, struck the backs of our heads and knocked us out.

*Five*

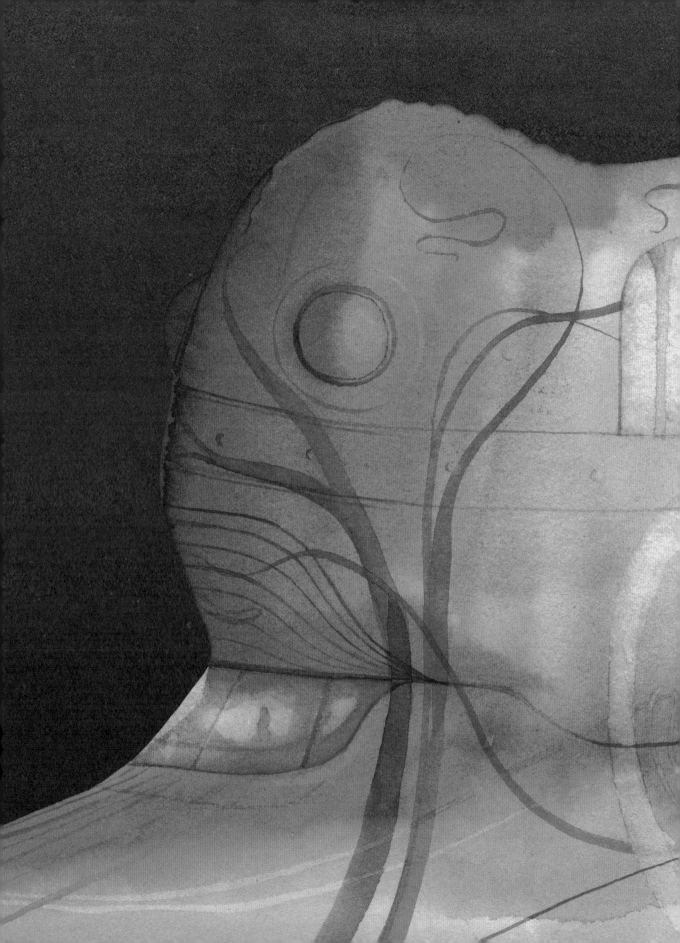

When I woke up, I was in a dark space. I couldn't see a thing—there was no light anywhere, which wasn't surprising, I guess, given we were in a submarine. But after a few minutes a network of faint lights appeared throughout the room. It was as if the space were outlined in light—lights along the walls, the ceiling, defining the contours of the room. And it was a strange light, too—something like electricity, but then more fluid than that, more liquid, the colour of honey.

I could see that Uncle Pierre was in the room, and Ned Land. They awoke slowly, Ned holding his head.

"You OK?" I asked.

"My head's killing me. And I'm gonna kill the guys who did this."

"Calm down, Ned," Uncle Pierre said. "You can't kill everyone on this submarine. We'll have to stay calm and find out where we are and who these men are."

Just then, two men entered the cabin. They were wearing suits resembling scuba gear, but the material seemed to be organic—shiny, smooth and very thin. The material covered every part of the men's bodies, even their hair and most of their faces. All that was visible was their eyes. They resembled sinister, human-sized seals.

They said something to us, but it was in no language I knew.

"Excuse me?" I said.

They spoke again, but their words made no sense.

We spoke to them in every language we knew between us—English, French, Spanish, Mandarin, Italian, Portuguese, even Icelandic—but they just stood there, looking baffled. And then they left.

A few minutes later another two men, also wearing the sealskin suits, walked in. One had three sets of clothes for us. The other brought in trays of food—fish and seaweed and some things I'd never seen. We were so hungry that we shovelled it into our mouths without asking. All I have to say is, it was good. But at that point I would have eaten anything.

As we were eating, another man entered. He was dressed like the others, but his face was uncovered. He had a thick black beard, dark eyes and a high forehead. He seemed to be about sixty years old, but he was fit and healthy—he certainly seemed a lot healthier than we were.

He stood there for a while, and we said nothing. We assumed that he, like the other crew members, spoke no known human languages. But when he spoke, his words were English and his accent English, too.

"How is the food?" he asked.

I was so startled to hear my language that I almost choked.

"Who are you?" Uncle Pierre asked. "Where are we?"

"And why are you keeping us here?" Ned demanded.

"I will answer the first question first," the bearded man said. "You can call me Captain Nemo.

You are aboard the *Nautilus*, a sea vessel of my own invention."

"What do you intend to do with us?"

"I intend to keep you here," Nemo replied.

"I demand you let us go," Pierre said.

At that, this Captain Nemo actually laughed—a big, mirthless laugh.

Ned's face was getting redder by the second. I knew he was about to say something rash, and he did.

"You better let us out, you bastard."

"I will do no such thing," Nemo said. "You tried to attack my ship."

"You've killed dozens of people, and I'll kill you!" Ned roared, and leapt at Nemo. Ned was a huge man, and extremely strong, but Nemo subdued him with ease. He stepped aside, pushed Ned into the wall behind him and quickly had Ned's arms in a kind of lock I'd never seen before. Hearing the commotion, two crew members came into the cabin and took Ned away, leaving us alone with Nemo.

I decided to allow Uncle Pierre to handle

the situation. I knew that in his adventures, he had been hijacked many times by pirates and had always managed a way to escape or negotiate his release. I was anxious to see how he dealt with this strange Captain Nemo. "Sir, do you intend to hold us indefinitely?" he asked.

"Good question, and politely phrased," Nemo said. "Thank you. The answer is yes. I intend to keep you here as long as you behave and observe the rules of the *Nautilus*."

"But, sir," Pierre objected. "Surely you can't keep us here for ever. We're not your prisoners. We have been sent by an international delegation to seek out the cause of so many sunken ships. We have been at sea for almost a month, looking. Now we find you, and it seems this ship might be capable of the attacks. I hope you can agree that we had a right to investigate the attacks."

"All of that seems quite fair. But you did try to sink my ship, and under the rules of war you are my enemies, and I can keep you until the war is over."

"War?" Pierre said. "What war?"

"Why, the war between man and the ocean!" Nemo said. "Don't you see? I am the protector of the seas! You, as a scientist, Professor Arronax, should know what I'm doing and why."

Uncle Pierre was incredulous. "You know who I am?"

"Of course I do," Nemo said. "I am an educated man, and I have read all of your books. Your study of the mating habits of the manta ray was particularly astute. I could quibble over some of the details in your texts, but why bother? Your work is brilliant, and I'm very glad that you're here. Having another man of distinction aboard gives me great pleasure. Would you like to see my library?"

Uncle Pierre, I could tell, was faced with a quandary. He was speaking to a man who might very well have murdered dozens of innocent men and women, and yet he was intrigued by the man's intellect, seduced by his flattery.

I decided to make the decision for him. I figured

we needed to see as much of the ship as possible if
we were to begin planning our escape.

"I would like to see the library," I said.

"Splendid," said Nemo, and led us out of the
cabin and down the corridor. It was the first
we'd seen of the vessel outside of our
tiny dark cabin. And immediately
it was apparent that this ship, or
submarine, or whatever it was,
had been designed and built
by an otherworldly kind of
brain. The hallways were much
higher than those of a standard
submarine, and the details and
fixtures were ornate, inspired
by organic complexity and
symmetry, and altogether more
beautiful and elaborate than they
had a right to be. It looked like
a nineteenth-century hotel, but was
modernized, too, with machinery and electronics
far more advanced than even a nuclear submarine.

When we entered the library, Uncle Pierre and I
gasped at the same time. It was a library to rival the

greatest in the world. There must have been 10,000 books there—along with myriad rare artefacts, and beautifully restored skeletons of dozens of ocean creatures. There were maps, precision instruments, shells and too many other fascinating objects and tools to count. In the corner, a beautiful organ stood, covered in gold and silver. The room was part scientific laboratory, part repository of knowledge. I could have stayed there for a year.

"Here's your book," Nemo said, pulling off the shelf Uncle Pierre's study of manta-ray reproduction. "Would you sign it for me?"

Pierre was close to blushing, flattered to have his intellect complimented by a man of even greater intellect. He signed the book for Nemo, and handed it back to him. And when he did, Uncle Pierre's face seemed to move from pride to shame. He was sucking up to a murderer!

But then maybe he wasn't a murderer. We had no definitive proof. After all, *we* had attacked *his* ship, and had been thrown into the Atlantic. He hadn't sunk the *Abe Lincoln*, and had in fact saved our lives. Maybe we had him all wrong?

"Nemo," Pierre said. "I have to ask you who

you are and what you're doing
in the ocean. I mean, this ship is
astounding. This library is the finest
of its kind I've ever seen. How did
you do this? What are your goals?
And, most of all, I must know if
you're behind the sinking of so many
ships and the loss of so many lives."

"My dear Pierre," Nemo said,
striding towards him. "I know we'll
be great friends. Your mind is a jewel,
and we will have much to discuss.
But for now you need rest. Let's talk
of larger things in the morning."

And with that, two crew members
entered the library and escorted us
out. We were given new quarters—a
comfortable room with two
beds, fresh linen and every other
accommodation we could want.
When we had situated ourselves,
the crew members left the room and
locked us inside.

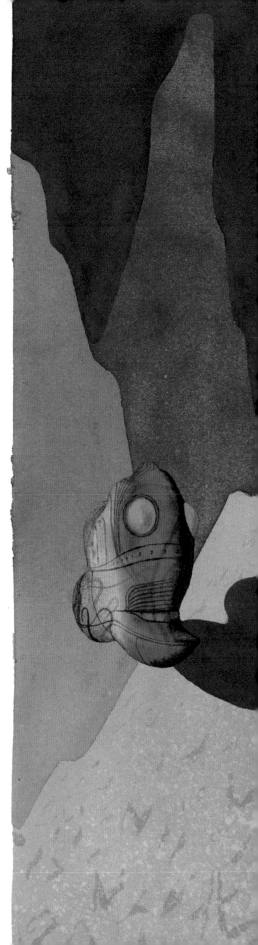

Six

The next morning, there was a card slipped under our door.

It said: "Captain Nemo requests the pleasure of your company on a trip of underwater exploration and discovery." It was engraved, as intricate as a wedding invitation.

"Very strange," Pierre said.

But, like every other thing that had happened or been offered since we'd found the *Nautilus*, we didn't have a lot of choice in the matter. We hadn't seen Ned Land since he had been hauled away, and could only hope he was being treated as well as we were. After we had eaten another delicious meal in our room, crew members escorted us to a strange compartment. A large porthole revealed that we were underwater, as a trio of huge pink jellyfish leapt by the windows. Along the wall of the compartment there were a number of the sorts of sealskin suits that they were wearing. On the floor, two sets of fins. Like

the sealskin suits, they resembled more perfect and organic versions of scuba fins.

"Ah, there you are!" Nemo said. He'd appeared behind us. "Pick a suit, and my crew here will make sure they are fitted properly."

I'd been scuba-diving a few times, and I thought I knew the basics of breathing underwater. But the suits that Nemo gave us bore no resemblance to anything I'd seen before. Like the crew's, they were made of what appeared to be all-biological material. They seemed to be sealskin, woven with strong thread of seaweed. We put our suits on and, I have to say, they were incredibly strange, as if I were wearing a smoother, stronger skin on top of my own. On our heads the crew members placed odd kinds of helmets—like standard scuba masks but far lighter and better-fitting. After we put on our fins, Nemo seemed satisfied.

"I will meet you in the sea," he said.

"Wait!" I cried. "How do we breathe?"

"Through the tube attached to the suit. How else?" he said.

I saw that there was a tube, as small as a zipper, attached to the chest of the suit.

"But where's the air tank?" I asked.

"You don't need one," Nemo replied.

And with that he pushed a button, opening a door to another, smaller compartment next to ours. He stepped in and the door closed behind him. Seconds later we saw him swim by the porthole. This space we were in was apparently a chamber that could be kept airtight, and the compartment next to it the gateway to the ocean. I was scared to be so far underwater—we couldn't see how far—and the enormous jellyfish didn't seem friendly—but I knew that Uncle Pierre wanted to follow Nemo, and I had no choice but to go along too.

We were led into the second chamber, and seconds later the steel door closed again and the door to the sea opened. I put the tube in my mouth, we pushed off from the *Nautilus* and were immediately swimming freely and breathing easily in the deepest reaches of the Atlantic. And though I panicked for a few seconds, thinking Nemo might have tricked us, soon I discovered that breathing through Nemo's suits was exactly like breathing actual air. It was a bit swampier, but otherwise it felt completely normal. Nemo was, I surmised, one of the greatest scientists the world had ever known. What was he doing hiding underwater? Why was he apart from the people of the world? I wondered. If only they could benefit from his discoveries!

He swam ahead of us, faster than I'd ever seen a man move. I now saw that his suit was outfitted with not two fins but one. His legs were inside a single tail, like a mermaid's, and he'd become so adept at using it that he moved as fast as a shark or dolphin. In fact, just then a pair of dolphins swam by, and Nemo, as if wanting to show off, swam off with them, matching their speed with ease. The

dolphins seemed to like the challenge and quickly turned around, seeing if Nemo could turn as quickly as they could. And he proved he could. They passed over my head at a startling speed—on land it would have been forty miles per hour. Soon the dolphins disappeared and Nemo returned to us, expecting us to be impressed. We were.

He nodded for us to follow. We swam in the direction of the *Nautilus*, where three crew members waited, carrying what appeared to be a number of large harpoon-like weapons. Nemo took one from them, about the same size and shape as a shoulder-mounted grenade launcher. He gestured that we, too, should take weapons and, reluctantly, we did. Then he pointed downwards, to what looked like a vast and dense underwater jungle.

At that point, I have to admit I was freaked out. I wanted to believe that Nemo knew what he was doing and wouldn't lead us purposefully into a deadly situation; but then again, I continued to harbour the suspicion that he was waiting for just the right time to kill us or watch us be killed. Maybe there was some deadly squid amid this seaweed? Maybe we'd soon be swallowed by a giant clam? I would put nothing past him.

When we reached the forest, the seaweed was as high as redwoods. The stalks were a hundred feet high, the fronds twenty feet long. I'd never seen seaweed longer than ten feet, and if regular seaweed was home to tiny fishes, what did this mean? What kind of fish would make its home in such an enormous forest? I tried to stay as close to Nemo as possible. I worried that at any moment a mouth would pop out from the fronds and swallow me in two gulps.

*Seven*

But Nemo had other ideas. It turned out this was a hunt, and man—a certain man, Nemo—would emerge victorious. After we had swum through plants of every colour, and had descended a gorge where the flora began to glow with the deep-sea phosphorescence known to creatures like the lanternfish, suddenly Nemo held his hand up, telling us to stop. He pointed ahead of him. At first I couldn't see anything. But as my eyes grew accustomed to the darkness, a shape emerged.

It was huge, ghostly white, with a long horn at the top of its head. No one needed to tell me what it was. I knew instantly I was looking at a narwhal. It was twice the size of any narwhal I'd ever seen or heard about. This one must have been forty feet long, not counting the horn, which added another fifteen.

Uncle Pierre turned to me, his eyes wide. I could tell this was the greatest thing he'd ever seen. If he could take a picture, or shoot some video of this beast, he would be the toast of the scientific world. He would change the world of marine biology, of oceanography.

But this wasn't to be. At that moment we saw the animal flinch, his eyes go wild. And then I saw that there was a giant harpoon sticking from its side. It was attached to Nemo's gun. Nemo looked at us, his expression gleeful. When he registered our looks of horror, he seemed surprised.

Within seconds the three crew members had shot the narwhal two more times and had subdued it inside a tight net. They were making their way back to the ship with the catch when Nemo shot again, this time striking a fantastic vampire squid of undulating colour. Like the narwhal, it jerked, oscillated and soon stopped moving. The crew came again and took the catch away. And this is how it went for the next two hours. Nemo shot a swordfish, a hammerhead shark, a giant seahorse and, in the most shocking kill of all, one

of the dolphins he'd playfully raced with when we first began the adventure. I was sickened.

When we got back to the *Nautilus* Uncle Pierre was outraged, and let Nemo know it. The moment we changed out of our sealskin outfits—which I then realized were probably made from actual sealskin—Uncle Pierre confronted Nemo.

"What was that out there? How can you kill such beautiful creatures?"

"Excuse me?"

"Are you some kind of hunter? Is this sport to you?"

"Sport? You call it sport! No, this is necessity. How do we eat if we don't harvest the ocean's bounty? You've been eating my food for days now. Where do you think it comes from?"

Uncle Pierre was apoplectic. "Certainly there's plenty to eat in the ocean without killing giant narwhals, hammerhead sharks and other rare species?"

"You call yourself a scientist? You're a fool. I hunted and killed a handful of fish, just enough for us to eat. Please tell me you know the difference between sustainably harvesting a few organisms to feed my crew, and the wholesale ruination of the oceans perpetuated by the world's fisheries? I am culling the oceans with great care and judiciousness. It's those corporate fishing enterprises that are killing the seas."

"Now I know it was you," Uncle Pierre said, his eyes narrowing.

"Of course it was me!" Nemo roared. "No other man on Earth has the brilliance to do what I did. No one has the courage."

And then I figured it out. It was Nemo who had sunk all those ships. He'd done it because they were all fishing vessels, all practising unsustainable methods. Until then I hadn't realized the connection between the ships he'd sunk. They were all involved in large-scale fishing operations—bottom trawlers, factory fishing ships.

"You killed all those people," Uncle Pierre said. "All those innocent men and women."

"Innocent!" Nemo practically spat the word. "Innocent? How can you call these murderers, these plunderers, innocent? They've erased ninety per cent of the world's coral. They've endangered hundreds of species! Entire ecosystems have been changed. The vast majority of the fisheries of the world are depleted. The oceans are filthy, barren, exploited, ruined! And it's all their fault."

"But you kill, too."

"When necessary."

"You kill people to show people that killing is wrong?"

"It's all you people understand."

"But you're human, too."

"Maybe. Maybe not."

"Yes, maybe not. Humans have compassion, and you have none."

For a second, Pierre and Nemo stared at each other, and in Nemo's silence, his inability to answer, Pierre gained new insight into Nemo's soul.

"What happened to you, anyway? What really happened to you?"

"You'd never understand," he said.

Then a look came over Nemo's raging face, something like recognition, something like regret. Uncle Pierre seemed to have hit on something— that no matter how sure and righteous Nemo appeared to be, he was unsure of himself. Perhaps he was unsure that he did, in fact, know what he was doing. But just as soon as that flicker of doubt appeared on his face, he regained his control and self-righteous anger.

"I am the law, and I am the judge! I am the oppressed, and they are the oppressor! Put them with that other animal," he said to his cronies, and stormed away.

Uncle Pierre and I were taken down the hall, and instead of being returned to our comfortable stateroom we were thrown into a different, much smaller compartment. And there we found Ned Land. He looked weak, famished. He'd been beaten in the face and his clothes were torn.

"And how was *your* day?" he asked.

*Eight*

We slept fitfully that night. We talked about how and when we would try to escape. We knew that we needed to. Nemo was brilliant, sure, but he was also a madman, and we no longer trusted him to act with any predictability or honour—even towards Uncle Pierre. Ned wanted, as usual, to attack the crew as soon as possible, to break out with all available haste and force, but Uncle Pierre convinced him that we needed to wait for the right opportunity.

"We must act now," Ned said.

"We must act wisely," Pierre countered.

Long after my uncle and Ned Land fell asleep, I stayed awake, thinking about Nemo and his way of looking at the world. He was surely not the first person to justify violence towards innocent people in the name of a purportedly greater cause. Wars were fought throughout history in the name of this or that idea, and those espousing these ideas were reliably certain of their moral superiority. But with most or all of these warmongers there was always contradiction and hypocrisy. Nemo wanted to ruin the commercial fishing business, but he himself was a hunter and killer of fish. He complained about the needless deaths of dolphins and sharks, but he murdered and ate them himself. And he admitted that people had a right to kill and eat the bounty of the sea—just not in reckless quantities. If humans went too far he'd be there to rein them in by slaughtering them the same way, indiscriminately, he said they were slaughtering fish. I thought and thought about it all night, and honestly I didn't get much clarity. Could any idea be pure enough to justify violence against the innocent?

And just when I thought I had exhausted my brain and would soon fall asleep, I heard a loud explosion just outside the *Nautilus*. I looked through the porthole and realized that we had surfaced, and were under attack. Uncle Pierre and Ned had woken

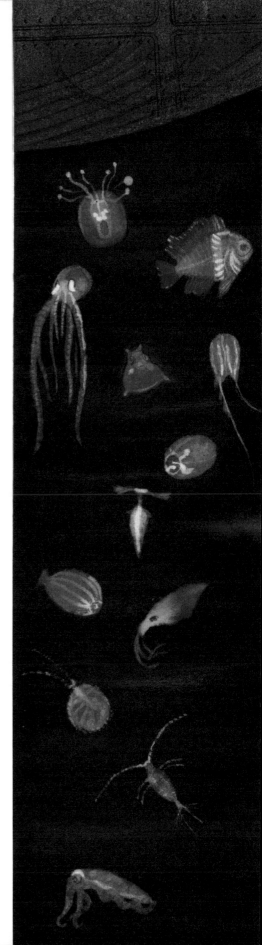

up with the explosion, and we each looked out from our own portholes.

I got a look at the attacker. It seemed to be a large factory-farming ship, where fish are caught in incredible quantities and then cleaned and packaged at sea. These ships could catch and process hundreds of tons of fish on any given trip, and often used mile-long nets that scraped the ocean floor, sweeping it clean of coral and all else. As I was watching the ship, I saw a small plume of smoke shoot from its bow. I thought nothing of it until, seconds later, another explosion rocked the *Nautilus*. They were shooting heavy artillery at us. Apparently this vessel was not only a factory-farming ship, but had also been retrofitted with cannons.

Just then, the cabin door swung open. It was Nemo. His eyes were wild.

"See? They're attacking us!" he roared. "Come with me!"

He left the door open and allowed us to follow him to the bridge. Uncle Pierre and I were left on our own, while Ned was escorted by two crew members.

When we arrived in the control room, a dozen crew members were manning their battle stations. It was the most advanced assemblage of computers, screens and lights I'd ever seen. It was beyond anything I'd seen in a science fiction movie.

Another explosion shook the *Nautilus*, and the lights went temporarily dim. I looked at Nemo, who was momentarily surprised, but then settled his jaw into something like amusement.

"Dive to thirty metres," he commanded.

"What do you plan to do?" Uncle Pierre asked him.

"I plan to sink that ship," Nemo said.

"But you could easily outrun it."

"So what?"

"So you're almost surely going to kill men if you sink it. Why not just flee?"

Nemo looked at Uncle Pierre as if he'd lost his mind.

"They attacked me first, Professor!"

"But you forced them to attack! You started all this!"

"You expect me to run from a battle? We are in a battle for the very survival of the seas, and I can't run from any fight."

Just then a crew member came to us. "We have a lock on the ship, sir."

"Attack at will," Nemo said.

"You can't do this!" Uncle Pierre yelled.

Nemo walked away. "I can and I will. Full steam ahead."

The *Nautilus* picked up momentum, a terrible momentum, and was heading directly for the ship. We were going so fast that the other vessel had no time to recalibrate their cannons. In seconds we were closing in on it.

"What the hell are you doing?" Ned yelled.

But to me it was obvious: Nemo would ram this ship, just as he did the *Abe Lincoln*, just as he had the dozen other ships he'd sunk. It seemed completely insane. Surely a man like Nemo, a scientific mastermind, could design torpedoes to sink any ship in the world. But instead he chose to attack them with something like a man-made narwhal horn, a giant knight's lance—as if this were a medieval joust! We closed in on the ship in seconds, and though I prayed we would slow down, we only sped up. It was the worst few seconds of my life, knowing we would collide with their hull any moment.

"You fool!" Ned yelled, and tried again to lunge at Nemo. A crew member raised a baton and rapped Ned's head. He dropped to the floor like a puppet.

The *Nautilus* was still picking up speed.

"Hold on!" Nemo hissed. The crew were all belted to their chairs. They'd been through this before. But we hadn't, and we weren't tethered to anything.

The impact was catastrophic. Ned and I flew across the room and against the wall. The ship shook for what seemed like minutes. The lights flickered, the machinery groaned and squealed. When it stopped, my skull was ringing and I'd dislodged at least three teeth. I spat them out and tasted blood. I looked up to see Uncle Pierre similarly injured. Ned was unconscious.

But Nemo was standing, his eyes happily watching the results of the attack. The *Nautilus* quickly reversed itself, the damage done, and positioned itself to watch the other ship sink.

Our victim was split in two, a toy broken in half. Fiery explosions burst from all parts of the ship. Men ran everywhere, trying to get to life rafts, trying to help those injured by the blasts. But for many it was already too late. The surface of the ocean was littered with corpses.

"Get closer and dive," Nemo ordered.

Soon we were within 200 yards of the wreck. It became obvious that Nemo wanted to see it fall to the bottom of the sea. Soon he got his wish. We saw the front half of the ship list and crash into the sea, and then slowly take on water. It fell in front of our window like a stone, its portholes filled with faces screaming. Then, seconds later, the back half of the ship sank—this time faster, as if it were being pulled to the ocean floor by some unseen force. Everywhere around the wreckage were men, parts of men, tools of men, all fading into the darkness of the ocean's floor. And then we saw something that probably made Nemo feel justified in everything

he'd done—from the falling wreckage a net, recently lifted by the fishermen, opened up and thousands of fish were freed. Most were already dead but a few were alive and they swam off, darting in every direction, silvery and catching the light from above, the effect like underwater fireworks.

When we surfaced again we saw a vast array of wreckage floating on the surface—anything that had been detached from the ship and could float. There were crates, tyres, mattresses, even a plastic bathtub. And we saw six large lifeboats, all filled with men. By my estimate twenty men had died in the attack, and sixty had survived.

"If you attack those lifeboats," Uncle Pierre said, "I swear I will fight you to the death. You've lost all sense of the meaning of life, sir. You're no longer a man. You're a savage. You're a senseless beast. You have no honour. No dignity. You say you're a man of science but you're nothing of the kind. You're a philistine. You're a caveman, ruled by anger and id."

Nemo turned on him, his eyes fixed and vibrating, and then walked away. Over his shoulder he gave one last command, "Chart a course due north," and disappeared into his cabin.

The lifeboats were left alone and those men, I hope, survived. But too many had died that day, and it became clearer than ever that Nemo had to be stopped, and immediately.

# Nine

We were locked into our cabin again, and there we stayed for the next many days. The ship was underwater most of the time, and it was impossible to keep track of hours and the passing of nights. Soon we had no idea how long we'd been there.

Meanwhile, the activity in the ship seemed to have slowed down. On the first day we were brought our meals three times, as usual. But the second day we were given only one meal. On the third day, nothing. The usual bustle outside the cabin and overhead gave way to a strange silence.

"We have to get out, and get out soon," Ned Land declared. And for the first time since we had all left Brooklyn together on the *Abraham Lincoln*, my uncle agreed.

We made a plan to break out of the cabin and make our way to the auxiliary ship. It would be that night, when we assumed the majority of the crew would be asleep.

Ned pulled the cords that circled the room, and the room went dark. Using a knife, Ned did reckless surgery on the door lock until it sprang open. We were free. But not quite. We had many obstacles before we could get to the boat, and liberating the boat from the *Nautilus* would be a feat in itself.

We tiptoed down the corridor, and soon were assaulted by a strange moaning. It was like a great beast in the throes of death. As we got closer, I could tell the sound was coming from the library, and it came from no animal, but a man. It was Captain Nemo himself, playing the organ and wailing a horrible and unrecognizable tune. It was such a frightening sound that an exclamation of worry escaped me. Uncle Pierre turned to me, urging me to stay quiet. Then he nudged me forwards; given I was the smallest, I peered in first. Nemo was there, playing the organ with sorrowful abandon. His movements were wild, as if he were drunk or simply beyond hope. Next to him was a picture within a humble frame, of a woman and child. The woman was elegant, smiling with warmth and confidence. The boy on her lap was about seven, black-haired and bright-eyed. He looked like Nemo

himself, and just as I began to put it all together—there was something beyond the survival of the oceans that drove Nemo to this state—the *Nautilus* shook violently, throwing all three of us past the library's doorway.

We continued down the corridor, and I noticed my uncle pause for a second beyond the library's doorway. I knew he was thinking of all the books and artwork and tools Nemo had accumulated, the collection priceless and irreplaceable. What would happen to all of it? The ship was being commanded by a madman, so it seemed likely that it would end up on the bottom of the sea. But it had happened countless times in history—one man's fury could consume centuries of human progress and beauty. Nemo had lost his family, how we would never know, but this was clearly most or all of his motivation, the source of his rage, his inability to care about the suffering of others. And now he had gone from angry to inconsolable. There seemed to be nothing we could do but escape.

To get up to the top of the ship we had to scale a three-storey circular staircase, and it was positioned dangerously close to the command centre of the ship. We knew that we had no option but to get up as fast as possible. The plan was for me to go first, with Uncle Pierre after me and Ned after him. They didn't need to say it, but it seemed clear that the plan was that if Ned needed to turn and fight off members of the crew, he was ready to sacrifice his life to save ours. And that's when I understood that a man's demeanour means nothing compared with his deeds. Ned was ornery, moody and generally disagreeable. But he was the bravest and most honourable man I've ever known.

We started up the stairs, and with my first step I heard the creak of metal. It was almost deafening. It seemed impossible that my own step could make so much noise. I figured right then that we would be caught. There were at least fifty more steps to get to the top—the whole crew would hear us before we'd got anywhere. But as we all stood stock-still, the sound of straining metal came again. And again.

We all looked at each other, dumbfounded. But then I saw on Uncle Pierre's face a sign that he knew what was happening.

"Maelstrom!" he whispered.

As if on cue, as if all the sailors on the ship were thinking the same thing, "MAELSTROM!" they yelled. Crew members all over the *Nautilus* yelled it again and again: "MAELSTROM!" "MAELSTROM!" "MAELSTROM!"

"Move!" Ned said to me, and I flew up the steps.

We were at the top of the stairs in seconds, and we darted to the lifeboat. It was small, just big enough for the three of us—Nemo hadn't expected ever to abandon this ship. The lifeboat was held in a small, enclosed area, like a torpedo chute. When we made it there, we could be sure that we weren't being heard.

"We must be off the coast of Norway now," Uncle Pierre said. "There's a vortex there, like a swirling

black hole of water, and we must be close to it."

"That's a maelstrom?" I asked.

"That's a maelstrom," Pierre said.

"Dammit!" Ned muttered as he loosened the bolts of the boat. "No way out of one of those but through it."

Uncle Pierre looked at me for a long moment. It was as if he knew that our chances of survival were slim, as if he wanted to say "sorry" and "good luck" and "I love you" all at once. But he said nothing.

"Let's go!" Ned said. The boat was free. We shot out of the *Nautilus* and into the open ocean. Even though it lasted only a few seconds, I'll never forget what I saw. It was exactly as Uncle Pierre described—a giant, swirling vortex.

The water was obsidian and night blue, foaming and spinning like an inverted marine tornado. I saw all that it was taking in—pieces of other ships, docks, sand, fish, even a grey whale who was lifting his head from the water as if looking to anyone or anything for salvation. It was the worst thing I'd ever seen, all of those ships and sea creatures heading to the bottom of the sea.

Just then, something hit me on the back of the head and I lost consciousness.

# Epilogue

You probably thought I would die. I did, too! But I didn't die. I woke up on the floor of a small house, with a roaring fire burning nearby. I tried to lift my head and the pain was extreme. I dropped back to the ground.

Sitting in chairs around me were Uncle Pierre and an older man, a fisherman who I would soon learn was the owner of the house.

Uncle Pierre caught my eye. "You awake, Con?"

I nodded.

"This is Erik, a fisherman," he said, nodding at the old man. "He found us floating on a piece of that boat. He rescued us and brought us here."

I looked up at the old man and tried to nod to him in thanks. The effort was too much, though, and I passed out again.

We stayed in Erik's house for the next four or five days. We slept, ate some kind of herring soup and recovered. We pieced together what had happened to us, were astonished that we survived and wondered what had happened to Ned Land. After two days of rest and recuperation, we heard a radio report about a man being found clinging to a piece of debris. He'd been washed up on the coast of Greenland. He was described as "red-haired, burly and babbling incoherently". We knew it was Ned Land. We were very glad he'd survived, though we never really had any doubt. The man is indestructible.

When Uncle Pierre and I were well enough to be up and about, we arranged to be brought to Oslo, and from there we flew back to New York. In New York, Uncle Pierre and I spent a week talking to everyone from the State Department to the United Nations to the CIA. Everyone wanted to know what we'd seen, but when we told them, though, no one believed us. We told them about Captain Nemo, the most brilliant and diabolical man we'd ever known. We told them about the *Nautilus*, the most advanced and ingenious vessel ever devised. But none of it made sense to them, and we had no proof. The *Nautilus* was presumably swallowed up in that maelstrom and had not been found. In fact, it was never found. Not a trace of it. There would never be proof of what Nemo had done. And so, every time a ship goes down anywhere in the world, we're left to wonder, was it the work of some terrible monster of the sea? Can we ever understand the mind of whatever creature would wreak this kind of havoc on the world? Will it ever happen again?

And I know the answers are yes and yes and yes.

# WHERE IS THIS STORY FROM?

Jules Verne was a French writer who was born in 1828 and died in 1905. He is widely credited with inventing the genre of science fiction. He also wrote *Journey to the Centre of the Earth* and *Around the World in Eighty Days*. He did a pretty incredible thing with *Twenty Thousand Leagues Under the Sea*. When he wrote the book, submarines didn't really exist. There were some prototypes, but no models in practical use. So everything he imagined in the original book was very, very ahead of its time. He had a big interest in science, and he was able to combine that with wonderful storytelling skills to conjure exciting adventures that managed to educate readers about scientific progress and unknown parts of the world. For these reasons he's one of the most famous and well-read writers the world has ever known. I have loved *Twenty Thousand Leagues Under the Sea* for decades, so when I was asked to retell a well-known story, I was sure of what I wanted to do. I would adapt Verne's classic undersea adventure, though—and I thought I was pretty clever here—I would be telling the story from the point of view of the giant squid. The problem is, there is no giant squid in *Twenty Thousand Leagues Under the Sea*. As with many classic stories and myths, many people have forgotten the essence of Verne's story. Every time I told someone I was going to tell a version of *Twenty Thousand Leagues* they would say, *Oh, that giant squid always scared me so bad!* This happens with certain stories—with the passage of time we forget them, we distort them, we invert them. We've done the same thing with Mary Shelley's *Frankenstein*. We forget that the doctor-inventor at the core of the book is named Frankenstein, and that his creation is nameless. We forget that the book is about the motivations behind and implications of Dr Frankenstein's twisted creation, not so much about about the creation itself. And so when I reread *Twenty Thousand Leagues Under the Sea*, I was re-educated about what the book was really about—it wasn't about man versus squid. What was it about, then? Well, I hope I got at that in the version that you have just read.

About this version: it is not meant to be any kind of definitive distillation of Verne's book. It is a personal and idiosyncratic take on it. And it's far shorter. The original tale was about 400 pages long, and this is a tiny fraction of that length. My hope is only that this abbreviated glimpse into, and updated version of, the original might intrigue a reader enough to bring them to Verne's inimitable text.

D. E.

# THE CREATORS OF THIS BOOK

DAVE EGGERS is the author of many books for adults and a few for young people, including *The Wild Things*. He is the co-founder of 826 National, a network of writing, tutoring and publishing centres for youth. A sister centre, The Ministry of Stories, opened in East London in 2010.

FABIAN NEGRIN was born in Argentina in 1963 and from when he was fifteen years old he drew every day, sometimes all day. He came to Italy more than twenty years ago and has now illustrated and written about a hundred books for children in Europe, Asia and America. He has a son and lives in Milan.

SAVE THE STORY is a library of favourite stories from around the world, retold for today's children by some of the best contemporary writers. The stories they retell span cultures (from Ancient Greece to nineteenth-century Russia), time and genres (from comedy and romance to mythology and the realist novel), and they have inspired all manner of artists for many generations.

Save the Story is a mission in book form: saving great stories from oblivion by retelling them for a new, younger generation.

THE SCUOLA HOLDEN (Holden School) was born in Turin in 1994. At the School one studies "storytelling", namely the secret of telling stories in all possible languages: books, cinema, television, theatre, comic strips—with extravagant results.

*This series is dedicated to Achille, Aglaia, Arturo, Clara, Kostas, Olivia, Pietro, Samuele, Sandra, Sebastiano and Sofia.*

Just as we all are, children are fascinated by stories. From the earliest age, we love to hear about monsters and heroes, romance and death, disaster and rescue, from every place and time.

In 2013, we created Pushkin Children's Books to share these tales from different languages and cultures with younger readers, and to open the door to the wide, colourful worlds these stories offer.

From picture books and adventure stories to fairy tales and classics, and from fifty-year-old bestsellers to current huge successes abroad, the books on the Pushkin Children's list reflect the very best stories from around the world, for our most discerning readers of all: children.

For more great stories, visit www.pushkinchildrens.com